AF425042

Ma

An Infernal Sons Novella

Carol Dawn

Ma

ALL RIGHTS RESERVED. THIS BOOK OR ANY PORTION
THEREOF MAY NOT BE REPRODUCED OR USED
WITHOUT THE EXPRESS WRITTEN PERMISSION
OF THE PUBLISHER EXCEPT FOR THE USE OF
BRIEF QUOTATIONS IN A BOOK REVIEW.

COPYRIGHT © 2020 CAROLYN JACOBS (CAROL DAWN)

ALL RIGHTS RESERVED

PUBLISHED BY CAROLYN DAWN JACOBS

COVER BY CAROLYN DAWN JACOBS

ANY REFERENCES TO HISTORICAL EVENTS, REAL
PEOPLE, OR REAL PLACES ARE USED FICTITIOUSLY.
NAMES, CHARACTERS, AND PLACES ARE PRODUCTS
OF THE AUTHOR'S IMAGINATION.

Dedication

To those who think you're too 'old' for new love, this is for you.

Chapter One
Ma

I look around my backyard at my family. Not just Landon and Logan, but all of the Infernal Sons and their families. I smile at my oldest grandchild, Sophia, as she runs around circles before falling.

Sophia isn't my grandchild by blood, but by love. She belongs to Bella. Chains woman. He adopted her not too long ago and officially became her daddy. He's always been her daddy, but now it's just on paper, as well. Now Bella has another little blessing growing inside of her that I just can't wait to meet.

My other grandchildren, Brendon, and little Daisy, are sleeping on a blanket next to their mama's.

Brendon is Thea and Trigger's adopted son. His birth mother, Thea's sister, died moments after Brendon was born due to a car crash. Sadly, the boy will never know his mom, but Thea is always telling Brendon, and everyone else who will listen, just how wonderful her sister was.

Then we have Daisy. She's the youngest, just over a month old. She belongs to my boy, Landon, and his wife, Rose. Daisy is my only grandchild connected to me by blood, but I don't love her any more than I do the others.

I feel a moment of sadness as I think about everything that Sam has missed. Sam is my late husband. He used to be the president of the Infernal Sons. He was killed about eight years ago from an enemy of the club.

I close my eyes and imagine him here at this moment. I can hear him rushing Landon on the grill.

"Hurry it up, Bear," he would shout. *"If I don't get a burger or three soon, I'm going to blow away with the wind."*

I imagine him welcoming each new member of our family with open arms and sloppy cheek kisses. I imagine him embarrassing me like he always would with his public displays of extreme affection.

"I don't give a fuck who can see us, woman," he would always say. *"I love my ol' lady, and I don't give a damn who knows it."*

I feel the tears fall before I can stop them.

"Who do I have to kill?" A concerned Mason says.

I laugh and wipe away the tears. Mason may seem like the meanest man alive, but he has a kindness in him that no one can destroy. I don't mind calling each man by their road names, but I can't seem to bring myself to call Mason, Trigger. Or Landon and Logan, Bear and Hawk.

"Just old memories, dear," I say.

"Why are you crying, Ma?" Chains stops beside Mason.

"Oh, you boys can spot a tear from a mile away," I grump. "I'm fine. Was flooded with some happy thoughts, is all. Now, when are ya'll going to leave? I have a date tonight."

I'm bombarded with happy screeches from Rose as she abandons her spot next to the blanket and rushes to me.

"Oh, goodness. Really?" She says excitedly. "With whom?"

Before I can answer, Bella, Thea, and Slim all start bombarding me with questions.

What's his name? Where's he from? Do we know him?

I simply smile and shake my head.

"You don't know him," I start. "His name is Ace. He's what you young kids call a silver fox. We've been out on two dates already. Tonight will be our third. And, that is all the information you're getting out of me right now."

"A silver fox," Slim says, fanning himself. "I can't believe you wouldn't share such useful information with your son-in-law, Ma."

"Hey now," Logan says, wrapping his arms around his man. "You don't need such information, sweet boy. If you so much as look at another man with those sultry eyes of yours, I'd kill him."

I take a step back and look around the group in front of me. With one look at the rest of the men, I burst into laughter.

Standing further back in the yard, Landon, Chains, Mason, Ink, and Brick stand with their arms crossed and looks of murder on their faces.

"Happy for you, Ma," Logan says, kissing my cheek.

"You deserve to be happy," Slim smiles. "I can't wait to meet your silver fox."

Logan glares at Slim.

"What is it with you and silver foxes?" Logan asks him. "Do I need to dye my hair silver to keep your attention?"

"Not in the slightest, big boy," Slim smiles. "And, I love this jealous side of you. I think I may flirt with silver-haired men every day so that I can see jealous Hawk more often."

Slim must see something on my son's face because he starts laughing and turns to run. Only he's too slow. Logan catches him, tosses him over his shoulder, and walks into my house.

"Not in my room again, boys," I scold. "You have a

bedroom, Logan, use it."

"A date?"

I pull my focus from Slim's distant laughter to the enraged son before me.

"Yes, Landon," I sigh. "A date."

"With a man?" he growls.

"No, honey, with myself." I roll my eyes. "Of course, with a man. You just calm yourself down before I embarrass you in front of your wife. You're not too old for a good spanking."

One side of Landon's lips tilts up before he quickly gets it under control.

"I don't like it, Ma."

"It doesn't matter much what you like, now, does it?"

"You should have told me sooner," he complains.

"Why?" I ask. "So, you could run a check on him?"

He simply glares at me.

"Have you been taking lessons from Trigger, honey?" Rose asks. "Your glare game has gotten intense."

I laugh and tell my son to get back to the burgers. I know he won't ever be happy with me dating. He is his father, through and through.

But I do know one thing. I will keep Ace away from this pack of wolves until we know for sure that we want to continue as a couple.

Even then, I am a bit scared at my boy's reactions when they find out who he is. Not just Landon and Logan, but the rest of the Sons as well.

It's a good thing I don't plan on them meeting for another couple of months.

I'm pulled from my thoughts at the sound of a motorcycle stopping in front of my house.

Shit.

Chapter Two
Ace

I'm nervous as I pull into Patty Allington's driveway. For multiple reasons. I wasn't supposed to arrive for several hours. I knew her family was coming over today, and she doesn't want me to meet them, yet.

I understand why. It's going to be hard enough when they find out she's dating. Patty is practically 'mother' to the whole Infernal Sons club. It's the most family-oriented club I've ever seen. Apart from my own, of course.

I know that my decision to show up now might make Patty angry. But, if it were up to her, I wouldn't meet her family for another year. And I can't accept that. The second I saw Patty, I knew she was meant to be mine. It was a strange feeling.

I've had a few serious relationships in my past that never worked out. I thought that I was just going to spend the rest of my life jumping from one woman to another. A man my age should already be settled down with a family of his own.

My club is my family. But I don't want to crawl into bed with them at the end of the day and get lost in their scent. Those fuckers stink.

Patty, however, is an angel and smells fantastic.

She smells like home.

I remember the first time I saw her. I went to the grocery store to grab some milk, and she was on her toes, trying to reach for a box of crackers.

I saw it before I happened.

She managed to get the tip of her fingers on the edge

of the box and started pulling it forward. Only, she leaned too far and began to fall.

I didn't think. I just ran.

"*Woah!*" She gasped. "*Thank you, kind stranger. That would have hurt.*"

I remember being struck silent by her voice alone. It was like I had been searching for the sound my whole life, and the moment I heard it, I couldn't fully comprehend it.

"*You can put me down now, big guy,*" she said.

I didn't want to. I wanted to hold her in my arms for the rest of our lives. I wanted to toss her over my shoulder, throw her on the back of my bike, and ride off to our future.

Instead, I asked her if she would have dinner with me. She hesitated for a moment before agreeing. Over the weeks, we learned more and more about one another. She told me her late husband used to be President of the Infernal Sons. A club in which both of her sons are members of. One which has held the president's patch since his father passed away.

I knew at that moment that them knowing about me wasn't going to go very well, at first.

You see, I also hold a president's patch to a motorcycle club. The Fire Dragons MC. We've heard of the Infernal Sons, and they've heard of us. We reside in the next town over. Franklin, Ohio. It's about twenty or so minutes away.

Chains, The Sons VP contacted my VP when shit was going down with that Hernandez idiot. My Vice President does all the grunt work. That includes dealing with outside business. So, I've never come across any of the Sons before.

However, when they learn my name, someone is bound to put two and two together and figure it out.

I've been sitting in front of Patty's house for five minutes now. Time to man up and get this over with.

I walk to the front door and knock. Before I can even move my fist from the door, it swings open.

"Well, hello there, mister silver fox. It is so very nice to finally meet you."

"You've known about him for ten minutes, baby," someone says from inside. "And, do we have to go back upstairs for another conversation?"

The beautiful man standing before me fans his face. "Dear God, yes," he says, winking.

I can't help but laugh at the handsome flirt. "I'm looking for Patty."

"Oh, I bet you are, daddy. Come on in."

The young man is jerked back. I rush inside out of concern only to see him over a broad man's shoulder, heading up a set of stairs, laughing.

"Ma's outside," the broad man says. He turns around, and I see my Patty's eyes looking back at me. This one must be Hawk. "You hurt my Ma, and they'll never find your body," he warns me.

I nod, expecting nothing less than the warning.

"Through the kitchen there and out the back door." Hawk turns and races upstairs.

I chuckle and follow the directions. Without an ounce of hesitation, I open the back door and walk outside.

Spread out on the lawn is Patty's family. The first thing I notice is the small group of women lying on a blanket with their children. Then, I feel the glare of the group of men staring daggers in my direction.

I look until I spot the Hawk look-alike. If it weren't for the hair and eye difference, you wouldn't be able to tell Hawk and Bear apart.

Well, except Hawk had kindness in his eyes when he looked at me. Bear just has fire.

I almost feel concerned.

"Who the fuck are you?" Bear asks.

Based on Hawk and his man's reaction and the smile on the women's faces, they know who I am. I'm being tested.

Bring it on, boy! I was burning rubber before you were born.

Ignoring the concerned look on Patty's face, I walk up to the group of men.

"Name's Ace," I say. "I'm here for Patty."

"I know why the fuck you're here," Bear growls. "What gives you the right to come on my land without my permission wearing another club's patch?"

"Yeah, I knew your name sounded familiar when Ma said it," a clean-shaven man says. "You're Dragon Fire's president, right?"

I nod my answer.

"Name's Chains," he holds out his hand. "I've worked with your VP, Skull, a few times."

I accept his handshake.

"I guess I'll pull back my alpha side a bit," Chains laughs. "Skull says you're a good man. My Prez here, on the other hand, may take a bit more convincing."

I look at Bear and can't help but agree. I'm not sure I'll ever get his approval. Then I see the man standing next to Patty.

Well hell. My love for the women might just get me killed after all.

"That's Trigger," Bear grumbles. "Good luck. He's worse than me when it comes to Ma, and that's saying something."

I walk over to Patty and tilt her head back. Ignoring the warning in her eyes, I claim those perfect lips where every single Son can see. I hear growls and feminine giggles.

"You are asking for trouble," Patty says against my lips.

"I like trouble," I admit. "Makes life fun."

Patty laughs and pushes me away.

She walks around me and stares at Bear and the men beside him. I smile back at Trigger to make sure he's aware that I don't want dead.

"It's like this, boys," Patty starts. "Ace and I are in a relationship, and there isn't a damn thing any of you can do about it. So, pull down your panties, take those sticks out of your asses and get over it."

I want to laugh right along with the girls but remember the bomb standing behind me.

"That goes for you, too, Mason," Patty says, glaring at the man behind me. "I don't want to have to deal with any of your shit. Trust me to know that I know what I'm doing. And trust me to come to you boys if I was ever in a situation that was over my head."

No one says anything, and Patty sighs.

"Don't you boys want me to be happy?" She asks. "I see each of you starting a family of your own. I'm lonely, boys. So lonely sometimes that I don't want to get out of bed. Is that how you want me to live the rest of my life?"

She turns to her son.

"Would your father want me to be sad and alone?"

Bear doesn't say anything, but his face softens.

"He wouldn't, brother," Hawk says from behind us. "Pops loved Ma with everything he was. If he knew Ma was so lonely, he would do everything in his power to make her happy. I think this is a good thing. I don't think it's fair for you to expect Ma to stay alone for the rest of her life for fear of her forgetting about Pops."

"Oh honey," Patty walks over to Bear and wraps her arms around his waist. "I could never forget your father, Landon. Not only was he my first love, but he gave me you boys. Hell, he gave me all of you boys. But my life with Sam ended the day he was killed. I've mourned him for years, honey. I've mourned the life we could have had.

But now I need to live for the life that Ace can give me. I need to let myself love another man. To be loved by another man. Can't you understand that? I loved your father, honey. That will never change. But I think it's time for me to open my eyes and live again. Can't you be here for me while I do it?"

Bear looks down at his Ma and wraps her in his arms.

"Fuck, Ma," he sighs. "Why did you have to get all deep on me?"

Patty laughs. "Because your head is as thick as your fathers was. It takes more than pretty words to break through and get to the commonsense section."

A heavy hand lands on my shoulder and squeezes tightly.

"If you so much as make a tear fall down her face," Trigger whispers next to my head. "I'll make you beg for death."

I turn around and see the seriousness in Trigger's eyes.

"I understand," I say. "But, know this, if anyone was ever to harm her, I'll make your torture look like child's play."

Trigger stares at me for a long while before nodding and releasing my shoulder.

"That was some pretty intense eye contact there, silver daddy."

"Phoenix," Hawk growls.

"I mean mister fox," the handsome man grins at me.

"Goddammit, sweet boy."

"What?"

"You know what. Now get your ass over here and sit on my lap."

"I don't think I'll be sitting on my ass for a while yet, big guy. You almost broke me this last time."

"Way too much information, man," someone says. "I gotta get to the hospital. I'll talk to you all later."

"See ya, Brick," Patty hugs the man. "Call me later and tell me how things are going."

"Will do, Ma."

The man gives me one last warning look before leaving.

I get it. Don't hurt the woman or I get dead.

I admire how protective they are of her.

"Well, that was interesting," Patty says.

I smile down at her perfect face. "It was, indeed."

"How about I get my purse, and we can leave?" she asks.

I look around the yard and make a decision.

"How about we stay here?" I suggest. "Looks like you all got some meat on the grill already. Now is as good a time as any for your family to get to know me. It won't take them long to realize how much I love you."

"You love me, huh?" she asks.

"Sure do, pretty lady," I admit. "Sure do."

Patty looks around at her family before returning her gaze to me with a smile.

"Well, if you can take those silent threats from Mason, I guess you're good enough to keep."

I nip at her ear.

"Of course, there is the matter of those babies," I say.

She looks at me, curiously.

"And what is that?"

"I'm having a tough time not walking over there and picking each one up for some old man cuddles. Which one is the safest bet to go to first? That tiny little girl?"

Patty tosses her head back and laughs.

"Well, that little girl just happens to be Landon's daughter."

"Oh, okay. I'll work my way up to her. What about the baby boy?"

Patty tries to hold back her giggle.

"Uhm, that one's Masons."

Well fuck! I'll probably never cuddle that one.

"Miss tumble?" I ask, nodding to the little girl who keeps trying to run only to fall.

"That is Sophia. She's Bella and Chains. A good safe bet to steal cuddles from her first."

I kiss Patty's forehead and make my way to the man now holding Miss Tumble.

"Oh, and Ace," Patty says.

I turn and give her my full attention.

"I love you, too, you know?"

I smile. "I know," I say. "How could you not?"

She picks up a pack of bread and tosses it at me, which causes Miss Tumble to laugh.

"Men," Patty grumps. "The lot of ya need your heads fixed."

I laugh and turn back to Miss Tumble and Chains.

It might take a little while to be entirely accepted into this family, but I'll work my ass off to do it. Anything to make my woman happy.

Chapter Three
Ma

I'm not really sure Landon will ever be pleased about me dating.

"It's been three weeks since everyone first met Ace, and my boy still gives him the side-eye," I tell Rose.

"It's not that Bear's not happy with you being happy, Ma," Rose says. "He's just worried that you're going to get hurt. He has a hard time trusting anyone when it comes to the people he loves."

I sigh, knowing it's the truth.

"He's just a big softie, isn't he?" I grin.

"Just don't let him know that we know the truth," Rose giggles.

"So, how are things with little Daisy?"

Daisy is shy of four weeks old and is simply perfect.

"She's doing better," Rose smiles down at the baby in her arms. "The doctor says she has colic. It's still rough to hear her cry when there really isn't anything we can do."

"Not to mention exhausting," I remind her. "Just be patient. Colic eventually goes away on its own."

"Ma, can you tell me how you met Bear and Hawk's father? I asked my husband, but he just told me that all he knows is that you met when you were young."

"Oh, darling, Rose. I remember it like it was yesterday."

"Daddy, can I please go? I promise to be back in time for dinner."

My best friend, Sherry, and I have been dying to go to the drive-in theater. I'm not sure what we're going to watch, but since she got her license, we try to go out every chance we get.

"I don't know, Patty," daddy says. "Will there be boys there?"

"I'm sure there will be, but it's just going to be me and Sherry, daddy," I tell him. "We don't plan on bringing any boys with us or bringing any back."

I hope he lets me go.

"Come on, darling," mom says. "Let the girls go out for a little fun. You heard her promise to be back in time for dinner."

I wait while my dad thinks over his decision.

"Alright," he finally says. "But, you best not be a single second late."

Knowing he's being completely serious, I nod.

I jump up and hug my dad before bolting off to my room to get ready.

Thirty minutes later, Sherry and I are pulling out of my parent's driveway.

"Can you believe that we're actually driving?" Sherry asks.

"Well, you're driving," I remind her. "Daddy won't let me get my license until I'm seventeen. But, still, this is all extremely exciting."

"Are you going to the dance this weekend?"

"I wish," I sigh. "I haven't been asked yet."

"Well, I just know that someone will ask you. How could they not? You're the prettiest girl in school."

I roll my eyes. She's always saying that even if it isn't true.

"Bobby asked me," she continues. "He just walked into class today and asked in front of everyone. I could have screamed."

"You did scream," I laugh. "I was sitting right behind

you, remember?"

"It's like the whole world fades away when Bobby speaks. No one else in the world exists except Bobby and me."

I clutch my belt. "I sure hope you aren't off in dreamland right now, Sherry. You're swerving a little."

"Oh, sorry," she says sheepishly. "So, what are we going to watch?"

I grab hold of the subject change. Once she gets started on the Bobby topic, it's hard to get her off of it.

"I think I heard they're playing a moving about a teen wolf."

We spend the rest of the trip talking about what we think the movie will be like. Sherry's usually really good at predicting the end of a movie before it happens.

"Let's not park too close," I say.

"I agree. Let's grab a spot near the back before they're all taken."

After we find a parking spot, we roll down our windows so we can better hear the speakers on the polls.

"Hello ladies, do you mind if we park beside you?"

I look out my window to see the very handsome Sam Allington, parked right beside us.

"Oh, um."

"Of course," Sherry says, grinning at me. "We don't mind at all."

I have had the biggest crush on Sam Allington for years. And Sherry knows it. Last year I almost had the courage to go up and ask him if I could borrow a pencil, but I chickened out.

"If that's alright with you, Patty."

"Huh?"

"Were you even paying attention?" Sherry laughs.

I shake my head. I'm mortified that Sam was actually talking to me, and I completely ignored him. Not on purpose, of course, but that's beside the point.

"I was wondering if you ladies would like to join us for the movie?"

"We're already here," I say.

Sam laughs. "I meant in the back on my truck, pretty Patty."

"Oh," I breathe. "The...uhm...with..."

"What she means," Sherry interrupts. "Is that we would love to."

I nod my head. My goodness. Where are my words?

"Hey, Patty."

I look behind Sam and see his best friend smiling at me. So, now I'm not only making a fool of myself in front of my crush, but Sherry's too.

"Hey Bobby, how's it going?"

"Oh, she does speak," Sam says.

Sherry laughs at my red face.

"Come on, Patty. Let's hop in the back of Sammy's truck and watch this movie."

My heart is racing a million miles per second, my face is on fire, my brain is melted, but I do what I'm told. Before I have a chance to do it myself, Sam opens my door and helps me out.

"Bobby, can you turn the truck around?" Sam throws Bobby a set of keys.

Once the truck is in the right position, we all climb in the back and watch the movie. Of course, Sherry had the ending predicted before half of it was over. And I honestly don't remember most of what happened because Sam was sitting right next to me. His legs were touching mine, his arm around my shoulder playing with my hair.

If there were a test on what they showed on that screen, I would fail completely.

"Say, Patty," Sam says after the movie ended. "Do you

have a date to the dance next week?"

In my mind, I said a full sentence. No, Sam, I do not have a date. Are you interested?

But I guess no sound came out of my mouth.

"She doesn't," Sherry said, causing Sam to laugh.

"Would you go with me?" Sam asked.

I slap my hand over Sherry's mouth before she can answer for me again.

I take a deep breath to give my head a chance to catch up.

"I would love to," I say. At least I think I said it.

"Awesome, I'll pick you up Friday at six."

The next thing I know, Sherry and I are back in her car and on our way to my house.

"Girl, you better learn to grow a pair if you plan on dating Sam Allington," Sherry tells me. "That man is badass now as a teenager. Just imagine how he's going to be as a man."

"I can't help it," I tell her. "It's like my brain goes all stupid when he's around. And besides, I bet he's going to grow up to be like his daddy. A quiet family man who spends his days in a nice suit while working at the bank."

"I doubt that, Patty. Something tells me that his future is one wild ride."

"She was right, of course," I tell Rose. "Sam grew up to be a wonderful husband, father, and man. But he wouldn't have been caught dead in a suit."

Rose laughs. "Did you go to the dance?"

"I did," I sigh. "It was absolutely perfect.

"Thank you for telling me your story, Ma."

"You're welcome, darling. Now, what do you say we make a meatloaf for dinner?"

"I say, that sounds delicious."

Chapter Four
Ace

I f looks could kill, I would have died a dozen times over by now. So far, I've won over everyone except Bear and Trigger. But I have a feeling that I'm about to have Bear on my side. I saw him crack a smile the other day when I kissed Patty's forehead.

"How do you feel about coming out to meet my brothers tonight, babe?" I'm leaning against the wall watching Patty bake a pie.

We've been dating for a while now, but my sole focus has been on making nice with her family. The Dragons have been badgering me every single day about meeting my new ol' lady.

"It's about time you invite me into your life, Matthew Harrington," Patty says, glancing my way. "I was starting to wonder if you were embarrassed by me."

I stare at my woman in shock. "Why the fuck would I be embarrassed of you, woman?"

Patty turns back to her pie. "Well, because I'm old," she mumbles.

I walk up behind my ol' lady and wrap my arms around her waist.

"There isn't a single thing old about you, woman," I say. "Do I need to show you how sexy you are to me?"

"Again?" She says with a smile in her voice. "Didn't you get enough already today?"

I turn her around and kiss down her neck.

"I'll," kiss. "Never," kiss. "Get enough of you."

Reaching down, I lift Patty up bridal style and head

towards her room.

"Put me down, you beast," she laughs. "You're going to break your old man back."

"I'll show you old," I grumble.

Reaching her room, I gently toss her on the bed.

"Stop," I say when she starts removing her shirt. "I want to unwrap my gift."

I lean in and slowly raise her shirt, kissing her skin as each inch is exposed to me.

"So beautiful," I whisper between kisses.

Once I reach her shoulders, I remove the shirt and kiss my wonderful woman on the lips.

"I love you, Patty." I enjoy the sensation of her soft skin as I caress her legs with my fingertips. "I love everything about you. I hate that we didn't meet early in life, but we still have many years to look forward to."

"Many more memories to make," she sighs.

Not knowing the words to say to express how much she means to me, I decide to show her instead.

Reaching down, I grab her pants and underwear and slide them down her legs, tossing them aside. My patience is quickly running out, but I need to taste my woman first.

I push her knees up and apart and take in my prize.

"You fool," she pants. "Stop your teasing, or I'm getting out my vibrator."

"I told you to burn those things, woman," I grump. "You'll only receive pleasure from your man from now on."

"Then get on with it, man, before I combust."

Laughing, I lean in and take a small taste of my favorite treat.

"Absolutely delicious."

No longer able to hold back, I dive in and give my woman exactly what she needs. Her body goes stiff, and her thighs trap my head in place, but I stop my tongue from making another stroke.

"Ace, I'm going to kill you," Patty whines.

"I want you to come with me, baby," I raise up and remove my pants. "I want to feel you squeeze my cock when you explode."

"Well, when you put it like that."

After tossing aside my clothes, I grip my cock and stroke it a few times. Seeing Patty spread out before me has my shaft dripping with need.

Not wasting any more time, I line my cock up to her waiting heat and thrust forward.

"FINALLY," Patty screams.

I can't help but agree. It's only been hours since I was last inside my ol' lady, but it feels like days.

I don't hold back. I thrust my hips back and forth, taking Patty for every ounce of pleasure she's willing to give me. Nothing has ever felt more perfect.

Knowing that I'm not going to last much longer, I reach down and quickly circle her waiting clit. Within seconds, Patty's pussy squeezes my cock with her release causing mine to burst forward without warning.

I throw my head back and roar out my pleasure.

Fuck!

I fall forward, catching myself so I don't squash my perfect woman.

"Yeah," she sighs.

"Yeah, what?"

"Yeah, I'll go with you to your club."

I smile and steal her lips in a deep, all-consuming kiss.

Hell yeah!

Chapter Five
Ma

I don't know why I'm so nervous. I've been around bikers for years now. But I can't help the butterfly's that are swarming my belly as Ace slows his bike in front of a building.

I'm completely terrified that his family isn't going to like me.

"I can hear you thinking, sweetheart," Ace says, shutting off his bike. "You have nothing to be afraid of. Everyone is going to love you."

Knowing that I'm being silly, I try and shake off the nerves and climb off the bike.

"You ready?" he asks.

"As I'll ever be." I grab his outreached hand and follow him into the building.

"This used to be a bar," he tells me. "When it closed down, the old President bought the building and turned it into the Dragon Fire club."

"How many members do you have?" I ask curiously.

"We're spread out into a few different chapters," he explains. "This is the Lebanon Chapter. We have five officers and roughly thirty patched brothers. But all together, we reach about five-hundred strong."

"I bet those runs get interesting," I say.

Ace opens the door and guides me inside.

"The fundraiser runs can definitely get interesting," he laughs. "But, for the most part, we leave huge get-togethers for big events. Today, you'll be meeting only a few of my brothers."

"Prez," someone shouts before the door has a chance to close. "Where the hell have you been?"

"And did you bring me back a pretzel?" another voice asks.

"Brother's, I'd like you to meet my ol' lady, Patty. Sweetheart, this is J-bird, Spider, Doc, and Texas."

"Just call me Tex, Ma`am, everyone does."

I smile. "It's nice to meet you, Tex, Doc, J-bird, Spider."

"Same here, Ma`am," Tex says.

"Please, call me Patty," I say. "Or Ma. That's what all my boys call me."

Doc grabs my hand and leads me to a round table. "We were just about to play chess," he says. "Do you know how?"

I nod my answer.

"Ma's on my team," Spider says. "Prez, did you stop and get me a pretzel?"

"No, Spider," Ace grumps. "I did not get you a damn pretzel."

"You see how mean he is to us, Ma?" Doc says, smiling. "He knows it's his turn to get the food."

I look back to see Ace grumbling to himself.

"We have a schedule," J-bird adds in. "Today is his day to pick up snacks, and we all agreed on warm pretzels from that little cart down by the library."

"I'll go get your fucking pretzels, you spoiled brats," Ace says.

He looks down at me, silently asking if I'll be okay. I laugh and nod my head.

With a final glare at his brothers, Ace turns and walks away.

But not before I saw that small smile pulling at the

corner of his lips.

The men pull my attention to the game of chess. Time to show these boys what it feels like to get beaten by a woman.

Chapter Six
Ace

Life is great. My men fell head over heels in love with Patty. Just as I knew they would. Bear finally talks to me about things other than my possible death. All of the Sons have finally accepted me into their group.

All except one.

"It's like this, Silver Daddy," Slim says. "No matter how many smiles you throw his way, Trigger will never return them. I've never received the mysterious Trigger smile, and he doesn't completely hate me."

I laugh and bring the dang flirt in for a hug. I don't think I'll ever get used to the young man and his nonfiltered flirting, but I take it all in stride.

Hawk sighs and takes a drink of his beer.

"I give up, sweet boy," he tells Slim. "But, if I ever hear you flirt like that with another man apart from Ace, I'll never let your ass go back to its normal color."

"Oh, you know what that means, Mister Silver Fox?" Slim looks towards his man. "Constant spankings."

Hawk is out of his chair and running before Slim finishes his sentence.

"He'll never learn," Bear says, watching his brother chase Slim around the yard. "Then again, I don't think he really wants to learn."

I laugh, knowing it's the truth.

"Listen, about Trig," Bear starts.

"Don't worry about it," I tell him. "I have a plan that might work."

"Good."

"Either that or he kills me."

I stand and walk over to Trigger.

"Listen, man," I start. "I understand your hesitation. I get that you just want to protect Patty. But, I'm here, and I'm not going anywhere. You can sit there and glare and threaten my life all you want to, but you are not going to scare me off. Get used to it, Trigger."

The man just stands there, glaring at me.

Not wanting to lose my temper, I take a step back and try again.

"I'll never hurt the woman," I tell him, suddenly tired of his mind games. "I'll never make her sad. I'll love her with everything that I am until the day that I die. As much as you may hate it, I'm here to stay, man. You can't push me away, no matter how hard you try.

Patty is my woman," I continue. "It's my job to protect her. It's my job to make sure her life is the best life she could possibly have. I need you to buck up and get over it, man. I won't let you or anyone else push me away from her."

I stare Trigger in the eyes, refusing to back down.

After a few minutes, Trigger nods his head.

"Good," he says.

I watch as he walks to his woman. When she looks up at him, his face transforms.

His edges soften, his eyes light, and his lips spread into a loving smile.

"He's a beautiful man," Patty says, stopping beside me. "He loves so deeply, Ace. He loves so strongly."

"Yeah," I agree. "I can see that."

I turn to my woman and kiss her smile.

Life couldn't possibly get better than this.

Chapter Seven
Ma

I walk until I find what I'm looking for and sit on the grass.

"Sorry, it's been a while. I just couldn't find the time to get away until now."

I look down, not expecting an answer.

"I never once complained about my life," I say. "I've had a wonderful life. But I thought that I would continue to age and die without ever knowing love again. But I've found it, Sammy. And I think you would approve."

I look up at the headstone displaying my late husband's information. Reaching out, I trace his name.

"I miss you so much, honey," knowing I can't stop it, I let the tears fall. "You would be so proud of our boys. Landon has really done well with the Sons. He's taking them to newer and brighter heights. And, sweet Logan has been by his side each step of the way.

Our family has grown so much. And it breaks my heart knowing that you haven't been here to witness it."

"He's always been with you, sweetheart."

I look back to see Ace standing behind me.

"He's not here physically, but that man never left your side."

I nod my agreement, wiping away the fallen tears.

Standing, I look down at Sam's resting place.

"I'm alright now, Sammy," I say. "I'm happy. Thank you for giving me such a wonderful life and a perfect family. I love you, honey. I miss you so much it hurts. But I'll be alright now. Please know that."

Ace wraps his arms around me, and I lean back against his chest.

A warm breeze wraps around us, blowing its soft kisses against my skin.

"That's an oddly warm breeze for this time of year," Ace says, smiling against my head.

"Yeah," I agree, sharing his same inner thoughts.

Sammy gives his blessing.

Ace turns me around and kisses me softly.

"What do you say we go live the rest of our lives?"

"I think that sounds perfect," I smile. "Let's go live, Ace. Let's go live."

The End

Note to Readers

Thank you so much for reading, Ma. You all kept asking if she was going to get a story. I didn't really have one planned for her, but then Mr. Perfect popped into her life.

Reviews are an author's best friend. It would mean a great deal to me if you would consider leaving a review on Amazon or Goodreads. Even just a few words would be amazing.

I like to do random giveaways. Sometimes it's a signed book, or sometimes it could just be a bookmark. You never know with me. If you would like to enter to win one of these random giveaways or want to stay up to date on all future releases, join us at Carol's Infernal Riders.

You can also join my newsletter to get the same information. And possibly early sneak peeks of future covers. http://eepurl.com/gKAehT

I know not everyone has Facebook. If you would like to reach out and contact me, my email is **authorcaroldawn@outlook.com**

About the Author

Carol Dawn was born in Maysville, Kentucky, USA, under the name Carolyn Jacobs. Carol is a stay-at-home mom where she spends her days making pb&j sandwiches, picking up toys, and giving her kids more cuddles than they want.

At the young age of five, Carol received a reading medallion for reading over twenty-one books in an eight-week period. So, her literary journey began. She wrote poems, songs, short stories and read many books.

Carol has a slight (MASSIVE) obsession with alpha male/insta-love romance books. If she isn't reading about them, she's writing about them.

When she isn't writing, reading, or playing mom, you will find her watching re-runs of Stargate SG1, Star Trek, cooking, coloring mandalas, or performing her favorite songs for her invisible audience.

Also by Carol Dawn

Infernal Sons MC, Series
Bear's Forever
A Very Beary Christmas
Chains` Redemption
Hawk's Choice
Trigger's Light

Audible
Bear's Forever audio

www.ingramcontent.com/pod-product-compliance
Lightning Source LLC
Chambersburg PA
CBHW030812170726
47995CB00011B/538